WORLD WAR II TALES

TERRY DEARY

THE APPLE SPY

Illustrated by James de la Rue

A & C BLACK
AN IMPRINT OF BLOOMSBURY
LONDON NEW DELHI NEW YORK SYDNEY

Chapter 1

Spiders and stories

Scotland 1940

Miss McLennan had a round, porridge-white face and little brown eyes. When she read us stories her little eyes grew wide and her voice grew excited.

Some of the kids in her class stared at her, mouths open, as if her words were dripping honey. Me and my brother Jamie thought she looked plain daft.

"'Mirror, mirror, on the wall, who is fairest of them all?'" the teacher read.

'It's not you,' Jamie muttered and I sniggered. I snorted too loud. I couldn't help it.

Miss McLennan slammed the book shut. 'Marie Bruce, go and stand in the corner,' she said and her mouth wrinkled like a breakfast prune.

I blew out my cheeks. She always picked on me. Jamie made trouble but I was punished. He liked that. Brothers.

The teacher went on, 'The wicked queen went into her most secret room and she made a poisoned apple.'

And the class went 'Ooooh!'

'From the outside it was beautiful, and anyone who saw it would want it. But anyone who ate a little piece of it would die.'

'Ooooh!'

You know the story. The queen pretended to be an old apple seller and visited Snow White, who refused to eat the apple. Snow White didn't live in war time like we did. We would have eaten a barrel full of apples.

'"Are you afraid of poison?" asked the wicked queen. "Look, I'll cut the apple in two. You eat half and I shall eat half."'

'Don't do it, Snow White,' Jamie cried out loud. Miss McLennan glared at him.

'Now, the apple had been made so that only the one half was poisoned. Snow White stuck her hand out and took the poisoned half.'

'Ooooh!'

Jamie listened, and it saved our lives.

No, really. Snow White saved our lives.

Chapter 2

Poisons and platforms

The class were sitting on the polished wood floor, legs crossed and arms folded. Miss McLennan said, 'Snow White barely had a bite of apple in her mouth when she fell to the ground, dead.'

Jamie jumped to his feet and said, 'An apple a day doesn't keep the doctor away.'

The teacher slammed the book shut and banged it on her desk. Her porridge face turned raw-beef red. 'Jamie Bruce, I am

9

sending you home right now. You cannot spoil story-time for the whole class. Get out. I will send a letter to your father.'

'And you can go with your brother,' she screeched at me.

We were out of the classroom faster than a sausage out of a frying pan when our cat was in the kitchen.

The September sky was a cloudless blue as we raced down the hill towards the harbour. 'Where are we going, Jamie?' I cried.

My ribbons were coming loose and my hair whipped around my face. Jamie's short grey trousers slapped at his legs.

'To the station,' he shouted over his shoulder. 'The Edinburgh express will be coming in.'

The station platform was quiet and smelled of the soot and oil from the locomotives that stopped there, steaming and coughing and creaking. The station-master, Mr John Donald, was smart as a pin in his navy uniform with brilliant buttons. His nose wrinkled when he saw us run onto the platform.

'Do you two rapscallions have tickets?' he asked.

'Yes,' my brother told him.

The man took a deep breath. 'Would it be possible for me to have a look at them?'

Jamie reached into his pocket and handed over two pieces of card. Mr Donald placed a pair of spectacles on the end of his nose and squinted through them. He tapped them. 'These are library tickets.'

Jamie shrugged. 'You asked if we had tickets.'

'Railway tickets?'

'Not yet,' I said.

But we were saved when the station-master looked towards the entrance of the station and said, 'Hello. What have we here?'

Chapter 3
Eggs and legs

Strangers. A man and a woman. They wore grey raincoats and brown felt hats and fine shoes. She wore a heavy tweed skirt and thick woollen socks. The man wore a dark blue suit.

Their pale, hard eyes scanned the platform and fastened on Mr Donald the station-master. The woman took a step towards him. 'Excuse me,' she said, and her voice was odd. Foreign.

Mr Donald gripped the lapels of his uniform and said, 'Yes, madam?'

'Tell me, porter, what is the name of this station?'

Mr Donald was a short man but he stretched as tall as he could and said, 'I am not a porter, madam. I am the station-*master*. And the names of all stations have

been removed. Then if a German spy arrives...' he said very slowly, 'they will not know where they are.'

The man stepped forward. He had an accent just like the woman. 'What a wonderful idea. Those German spies must be defeated. No?'

'No...I mean, yes,' station-master Donald said.

'We came here to Forres for a walking holiday,' the man said. 'Now we take the train to London.'

'This is not Forres,' Mr Donald said. 'This is – '

'Lossiemouth,' I said quickly. I met the eyes of Mr Donald and those eyes seemed to say, 'Thank you.' He had almost given us away.

'We got a little lost,' the woman said.

But Forres was 25 miles away. Jamie

spoke from the side of his mouth. 'They didn't walk here. A German submarine or seaplane dropped them off. They were rowed ashore in a boat.'

'You read that stuff in *The Wizard* comic,' I hissed. 'You think Miss McLennan is a Russian spy and you're the Wolf of Kabul.'

He looked worried. 'This is serious, sis.'

'You can't accuse people of being spies without any proof,' I said.

'But I do have proof,' he murmured. 'Look at the bottom of the man's trouser legs.'

Chapter 4
Butcher and baker

'They're wet,' I said quietly.

'They are...and it's a dry day,' he muttered. 'Look just below the knees where the water has started to dry.'

'There's a ring of white,' I said and started to understand. Jamie may be a clever detective but I'm not stupid. 'Wet with salt water...sea water.'

Jamie gave a small smile. 'They've stepped out of the sea. The woman's shoes are covered in salt too. A submarine or a seaplane put them in a rowing boat. They rowed to the beach but had to jump into the water and walk the last few yards when the boat hit the bottom.'

'But they weren't sure where they'd landed so they had to ask,' I said. 'Spies.' I leaned closer to my brother and whispered, 'What are we going to do?'

'Run and get the Home Guard and the police,' he said.

I turned and raced through the entrance to the station. I sped along Station Road and turned into the High Street. As I reached the little police box I saw Constable Grieve coming out. I snatched at his sleeve and babbled my story. '...and the express leaves at ten.'

If Constable Grieve had ever done any running it had been thirty years ago. But now he shuffled into a trot like a rhino and still found enough breath to

blow his whistle. 'Home
Guard...bring your rifles...get
to the station...German spies...'

Mr McKenzie the grocer said,
'I'll just get my uniform on.'

'No time,' I said. 'They'll be on the
express train at ten. Just bring your rifle.'

He vanished into the shop and came out a moment later, running up Station Road in his white apron. He was joined by Mr Mackay the butcher in his navy apron with white stripes and crimson blood, and Mr Bell the Baker, who always sounded like a man on a *Happy Families* card to me.

We could see the express steaming along the coast line. The men struggled to load their rifles as they ran. They dashed through the station entrance and by the time I got there the foreign couple had their hands in the air and three rifles were pointed at their heads.

Constable Grieve was gasping for breath, wheezing like the express train that was huffing down the line. The policeman couldn't speak. So I spoke for him. 'We arrest you in the name of the law.'

Jamie grinned at me. 'I've always wanted to say that.'

We were so pleased with ourselves. We would be on the newsreel at Buckie cinema next week. We had saved Britain from these evil Nazi spies, I thought.

But I was wrong.

Chapter 5
Smoke and signals

As the two spies were led away the express train hissed, clanked, roared, spat, screeched, shuddered, groaned and rumbled its way to the platform in a cloud of steam and smoke.

Constable Grieve would call the army to take the foreign couple away and question them. I didn't follow. I looked down the platform as the train crunched to a halt. No one got off the train today – not many people came to Portgordon. The train guard stepped off the last coach with whistles and flags.

The sea breeze blew away the steam cloud and I saw something that made my heart stop as still as the train. A man was walking along the track towards the train. He walked up the ramp at the end of the platform, opened a carriage door and climbed in.

He was thirty yards away from me but I was sure I had seen the white salt-stains on his trousers.

'Jamie!' I cried after my brother who was following the arrested spies. At that moment the engine gave off a whistle to warn everyone to stand clear.

'Jamie!' But the screaming of the slipping wheels drowned my voice.

The guard folded the green flag he'd been waving and climbed aboard the guard van at the end. The train began to move. I ran alongside, tore open a carriage door and pulled myself in.

They say that twins can 'talk' without speaking. They send invisible messages from their brains – a bit like wireless waves. Jamie swears he didn't hear me cry out. Yet he had stopped and turned around at the station entrance to look for me. He ran back just in time to see me jump on board.

He didn't know where I was going or why. I didn't even know that myself. But he ran alongside the train and caught it as the guard's van at the end went past. There was no door to open on the van platform. Just a handrail. My brother caught hold and the speed lifted him off his feet.

I leaned out and watched as he fell back. His feet struck the last few inches of Portgordon platform and he seemed to bounce up like a ball. The wind dragged at him and pulled him backwards, his grip slipping off the rail. The engine rushed past the signal tower at the side of the track. If Jamie's struggling body hit that he'd be crushed. If he let go he'd fall under the back wheels of the van.

Then I saw a large hand reach from the van and grasp Jamie's arm. The guard gave a strong tug and Jamie was pulled to safety a moment before the van reached the signal tower.

If he'd been killed with that crazy jump it would have served him right. But I was still pleased to know I wasn't alone on the train.

I just didn't know what to do next.

Chapter 6
Tickets and tracks

I knew I had to follow the man with the sea-water legs. He had to be a spy like the other two. I had to find him then tell someone.

The express train had ten carriages with a corridor that ran from the engine at the front to the guard's van at the back. Every carriage had about twenty compartments with six seats in each.

The first thing I had to do was find the spy. He couldn't escape until the train stopped. Then I'd have the railway police

– and Jamie – to help me. I wasn't afraid.
I should have been.

I decided to start at the front. I stared
into each compartment. Some were empty
and some held one, two or three people.
The spy wasn't in the first carriage.

In the second carriage I saw the third
compartment was crowded with a mother
and five noisy children. I smiled. That
solved one problem.

A ticket collector walked down the corridor towards me. 'Tickets from Portgordon,' he cried.

I smiled at him sweetly. 'I'm with my family in the third compartment. Mummy showed you our tickets before.' He nodded and walked on.

I found the spy in the last carriage before the guard's van. It was the carriage he'd jumped into at Portgordon. He hadn't bothered to walk through the train. He hadn't tried to hide.

He had fair wavy hair over a handsome face. He had taken off his shoes and rested them against the heater pipe that ran below the window. Suddenly the man looked up, saw me watching him and smiled.

The train rattled over the rails with a clickety-clack like a drum beat. I looked out of the window and watched the

fields and the villages rush past while the
distant purple mountains and moorlands
sat quietly in the morning sun.

'Good morning, little girl,' he said
softly. 'You will get tired standing there.
Come into the compartment with me.'

I turned round, icicle stiff and icicle cold.

Chapter 7
Locomotives and lies

I was safer in the corridor, I knew. A fly is safer in the sky but it still buzzes into the spider's web, doesn't it? I stepped into the compartment. He slid the door shut and pulled down the faded brown blinds.

'There,' he said with his handsome smile. 'That will keep the cold air out... what is the word you English use?'

'Draughts. And I'm not English. I'm Scottish.'

He bowed his head. 'Of course. I am in Scotland. I must remember. A good place for walking in the giant hills.'

'Mountains.'

'Mountains, as you say.' He smiled a cold smile. 'I got on the train at your little station. There was a lot of things happening on the platform. What was that?'

'Two German spies were arrested by the Home Guard,' I said.

He sighed then turned his pale, hooded eyes on me again. 'And you got on the train at there, did you not?'

'Yes.'

'You watched me climb on the train and then you jumped on. Why did you leave it so late? You could have hurt yourself.'

'I was watching the arrest. I didn't hear the guard blow his whistle,' I said.

'You were watching me. Are you following me?'

'No,' I said loudly. 'Of course not.'

'Where are you going?'

'Edinburgh. To stay with my aunt and uncle,' I lied. 'He's a policeman,' I added, wild as a Highland sheep.

The spy's eyes never moved from my face. 'And will he be there to meet you at the station?' He placed the suitcase across his knee and clicked the two catches. I was sure he was reaching for his gun.

If I said 'yes' then he would shoot me on the spot and throw my body from the carriage window.

I tried to speak. 'I... I...'

I was saved by the ticket collector. 'Aberdeen,' he cried from the corridor. I heard his footsteps coming nearer. 'Next stop Aberdeen.'

The carriage lurched as the locomotive slowed. The fields and hills outside gave way to rows of grey granite houses and greyer roads.

The spy reached into his case and wrapped his bony fingers around something inside.

Chapter 8
Aberdeen and apple

My mouth went dry. I looked out of the windows and saw the backs of shabby houses move past, slowly now. He had just seconds to pull that gun from his case and shoot me and throw me out of the window.

He spoke quietly. 'It is a long way to Edinburgh.'

I nodded.

'Did your family send you with anything to eat?' he asked. 'You have no bag.'

'No,' I croaked.

'I have plenty of food. I know you English are short of food in this war. The German submarines sink your food ships and leave you starving.'

'I'm not English. I'm Scottish,' I said, scared into talking stupidly.

'I forget,' he said.

The train brakes screeched and the carriage rocked as it drew up to the platform and stopped. He couldn't shoot me now, I thought. Someone might come into the carriage. But he pulled his hand from his suitcase and I gasped. In his hand he held an apple.

It wasn't a rosy or a golden apple and the skin wasn't shiny. It was green and a little bit wrinkled. I discovered I really was hungry.

'Aberdeen,' the ticket collector's distant voice cried as doors clattered open and steam hissed.

The spy's voice was low and kind. 'Here, young lady. You can have my apple.'

I took it and felt juices in my mouth. I raised it to my lips. I hadn't eaten an apple since the war started a year ago.

A door near the end of the carriage banged open. A boy called out, 'Marie? Marie?' He sounded like my brother Jamie. I'd answer him after I'd taken a bite. 'Marie?' he called and the door to the compartment next door slammed open. My mouth opened.

'Enjoy it,' the spy breathed.

The door of our compartment slid open so hard the blind wound up with a whoosh. Jamie stared in and saw me. 'No, Marie!' he cried. 'Remember Snow White!'

He jumped forward and knocked the apple out of my hand. It rolled on the floor.

The spy picked it up. He looked cross. My brother grabbed my wrist and dragged me out of the carriage.

'It's poisoned,' he said. 'And I don't have seven dwarfs to bring you back to life.'

That made sense. The spy wouldn't shoot me with loud bangs if he could poison me quietly.

Like I said, Snow White saved my life.

Chapter 9
Smiles and sandwiches

Jamie dragged me towards the guard's van. A man in a faded blue uniform with a face like Aberdeen granite helped me into the dusty brown van. There were parcels and baskets on the floor and a hard wooden bench to sit on.

'Wait there,' he said before stepping out to wave a green flag and send the express on its way. He climbed back as we rolled out of Aberdeen station. 'Now what's all this nonsense?'

'Mr Murdoch here doesn't believe me,' Jamie said quickly. 'He thinks we're just trying to steal a free ride to Edinburgh. He says he'll put us off at Dundee and let us walk back home.'

So I told my story and the guard listened with his lips set hard. 'He says he's a walker,' I argued, 'but he has a suitcase. He isn't wearing walking boots, he's wearing shoes. He doesn't seem to have a map. He

only knows he's somewhere on the north-east coast of Scotland. And he tried to poison me with an apple.'

'So why aren't you dead?' the man asked.

'I didn't eat it.'

'So how do you know it was poisoned?' he asked. Good question.

I looked at Jamie. 'Did you tell him about the other two at Portgordon?'

'No.'

I looked at Mr Murdoch the guard. 'We saw two spies on the platform at Portgordon. The police and the Home Guard there believed us and took them away. They were wearing the same sort of clothes and had the same salt-stains round their ankles. But this man came along later. The police missed him. You can check with the police at Portgordon.'

Mr Murdoch nodded slowly. 'I may

just do that,' he said. 'The last stop is Dundee in an hour. I'll give them a call. But if you two are lying to me I will wait till we are on the Tay Bridge and throw you in the river.'

Jamie blew out his cheeks. 'No, you won't.'

The old man leaned forward on his seat and hissed, 'No, I won't. I'll wait till we get to the bridge over the Firth of Forth and throw you in there. It's deeper.'

Then he did a really scary thing. He smiled at us. 'I have a packet of sandwiches. The wife always makes too many. Would you like some?'

'Are they poisoned?' I asked.

'Of course,' he said.

'Then I'll have two,' I said.

Jamie and I returned his smile.

Chapter 10
Storm and sausage

As soon as the train stopped at Dundee the guard hurried across the platform.

Three minutes later he hustled back into the guard's van and said, 'Next stop Edinburgh. The army will be waiting for him there. Well done, you two.'

He leaned out of the van, waved his green flag and gave a long, loud blast on the whistle. Then he passed us a brown paper bag and said, 'These are for you.'

We opened the bag and found a bottle of lemonade and mutton pies.

We drank from Mr Murdoch's tin mug and the hot pies vanished down our throats.

We hurried over the Tay Bridge and had crossed to the south side before Mr Murdoch told us its terrible tale. 'Sixty years ago, on a wild December night, there was a terrible storm. The wind was hard as a wall and fierce as a hungry dog. It chewed and tore at the Tay Bridge till the struts and spars began to crack. That's when the 7.13 train from the south headed out onto the bridge, picking up speed. The signalman waited to see the train appear on the north bank. It never did. The train had plunged in the river. Seventy-five people were on the train, poor souls. Not one of them lived.'

The old man's stories kept us amused for an hour or more. I forgot about the spy in the coach ahead. Suddenly Jamie asked, 'Is he really a spy?'

Mr Murdoch nodded. 'I phoned Edinburgh from Dundee and they told me they'd heard from your friends in Portgordon. They searched the man and the woman they'd caught. And what do you think they found in their suitcases?

'A gun?' I said.

'A radio?' Jamie added.

The guard chuckled. 'You are a bright pair. That's exactly what they found. They also found three hundred pounds in money...and a German sausage. Oh, they're spies all right. And dangerous ones too. The army will be waiting in Edinburgh when we get there at half past four.

You two must stay here till it's all over and our friend is arrested.'

I was annoyed. Jamie and I had found the spy but we were going to miss out on the fun of seeing him arrested.

I never did what I was told in school. I wasn't going to do what I was told now.

Chapter 11

Carriages and clowns

At 4:30 exactly we pulled into Waverley Station in Edinburgh. I peered through the smoky glass of the guard's van window. It was gloomy under the sooty station roof. There were few lamps lit because of the blackout.

The police were waiting and so were half a dozen soldiers. But you had to look hard to see them. They were half-hidden by the newspaper stalls and the coffee shacks and sandwich-sellers' trolleys.

Mr Murdoch opened the van door and gave one last warning. 'Stay here till it's over.'

The carriage doors opened and as the passengers spilled onto the platform Jamie and I slipped out too.

A man in heavy black boots and a cream mac moved forward. He was a plain-clothes detective, I guessed. They didn't want the spy to see a policeman in uniform and run for it before they could arrest him.

The detective stood by the door to the last carriage as people swirled past him like water flows round a rock in a stream. The spy didn't get off. The detective's face looked as if it were carved from wood...worried wood. He gave a signal with his finger, and two policemen and six soldiers clattered over the platform to the last carriage.

They were a mass of elbows and rifles
and boots and belts as the khaki clowns
all rushed to be first through the door.
There was a lot of shouting and arguing.

I saw the family from the front coach
with their mother whirling down the
platform. The baby was bawling, the

toddler was tumbling and the young ones were yelling.

A man walked alongside them trying to chat and cheer them up after their weary trip. He was just like any other father with a brood of bairns.

Only he wasn't their father. I had looked into that carriage and there had been a mother and five children but no father. The man with the children had his hat pulled down to shade his face. I knew it was the spy.

He must have known the police would be waiting for him. He had simply walked to the front of the train and got off at the other end.

I turned to Jamie. 'That's him.'

'Tell the police and the soldiers,' he said.

'They're jammed in the carriage. They're running up and down like rats in our barn.

He'll be out of sight before they get out.'

'So we'll have to follow him,' Jamie said.

And that's what we did.

The family crossed towards a sign that said the Glasgow train would be leaving in five minutes. The spy left them and walked quickly over to a porter with a greasy grey waistcoat and a battered cap. He spoke a few words, pushed something into the porter's hand, then looked at his watch. He turned and half-ran up the stairs to the street.

I raced across to the porter. 'What did that man say?' Jamie asked as I watched the spy's heels vanish over the top step.

'He asked if this was Edinburgh. I said, "Well it's not New York!" He didn't laugh. He just asked where he'd get the London train and I said platform six. Then he asked what time, and I said ten o' clock tonight. He looked a bit upset at that.'

Jamie grinned. 'We just have to keep him in sight till ten o'clock. Then he'll be back here.'

'But the police and the soldiers won't,' I said. 'They'll give up and go home. You need to go back and tell them to lay a trap.'

'Me?' Jamie asked.

'Yes. I'm the one who knows what he looks like. I have a better chance of finding him in the crowds. Hurry.'

Jamie looked worried but he turned away. I raced up the steps after the spy into the gloomy, smoke-dark streets.

Chapter 12

Brownies and boots

I had only been to Edinburgh twice – once on a school trip to the Castle and once with the Buckie Brownies to a jamboree. But I knew that the old town and the castle were on the left when I came out of the station. The new town with Princes Street and all the modern shops was on the right.

When I reached the road I peered out towards the old town but couldn't see him. He only had twenty seconds' start but I had lost him already. Then

I heard the sharp blast of a taxi horn. The spy had looked to his left and stepped off the pavement. In Germany they drive on the right. He forgot we drive on the left.

I turned sharply towards the noise and saw the man jump out of the path of the taxi. He was headed for the wide streets of the new town. I followed him up Princes Street and ducked into doorways when he stopped to look back. Then he turned up a side street. I raced to the corner and was just in time to see him vanish into a doorway.

I followed and squinted up at the sign above the door. 'The Stag Inn', it said. He was planning to spend three hours in a pub. They wouldn't let me in.

I crossed the road and found the doorway to a cobbler's shop that seemed

to have closed down. I sat back in the shadows to wait.

The ground was cold and my thin school dress didn't keep out the chilly, damp Edinburgh air.

As I shivered I almost wished I was in Miss McLennan's cosy classroom again, listening to soppy stories of princesses, giants, fairy godmothers, wicked witches and frog princes. But my story was better.

A distant clock chimed every quarter hour. When I heard it strike half past nine I rose to my feet. My legs were stiff as a witch's broomstick and I couldn't feel my feet. I stamped on the pavement and slapped my arms till they warmed.

I almost missed him. He slipped quietly out of the pub and started to walk back down towards the station. I followed.

The man swung his suitcase by his side and headed for platform six. I saw figures step out of the shadows. The spy stood on the platform and waited, silently. Then he seemed to sense the men moving towards him. I saw my idiot brother at the front of the gathering group.

The spy snapped open his case and slipped something into his pocket. I knew it was his gun. He would shoot Jamie. Mum would kill me if I let that happen.

A soldier's steel-studded boot sparked on the stone path to the platform. The spy swung round and pulled out his gun. Six rifle-bolts clattered as the soldiers put bullets in the breeches of the rifles, ready to fire.

The detective stepped forward. He spoke quietly. 'Put down the gun. There are twenty rifles aimed at your head right now.'

The spy shook his head sadly. He threw the pistol to the ground. A policeman ran forward and picked it up while another snatched the suitcase. The detective snapped handcuffs on the German and led him away.

That should have been the end of our adventure...but it wasn't quite.

* * *

The detective's name was Inspector Nixon. He took us to the police station. He told us our parents had been told about our journey and we were heroes back in Portgordon. We could sleep in the police cells and go home the next day.

We walked through the police station,

down the shabby green corridors until we came to the cell that held the spy. The prisoner turned and pleaded. 'My apples,' he said. 'You have my apples in my case?'

'I have,' Nixon said.

'May I have them. Please? Fetch my apples and I will tell you everything. The codes, the drop-off points, the names of agents already in your country. The whole of the German spy network. Anything.'

'I wonder where we can find two wrinkled apples at this time of night?' Jamie asked quietly.

'We'll give him his own apples,' Nixon shrugged. 'Can't be any harm in that.' He reached into the suitcase and took the fruit out.

'Oh, but you can't do that!' Jamie said.

Nixon frowned. 'Why not?'

'Because they're poisoned. One bite

and he'll be dead. You won't get a word out of him.'

Nixon slapped his own forehead angrily. 'Of course,' he cried. 'All spies carry poison with them. They will kill themselves so they don't have to talk and betray their country. Jamie, you are a genius.'

I scowled. 'No. He just listens to too many fairy tales like Snow White.'

Jamie smirked like Happy the Dwarf.

I just felt Grumpy.

Epilogue

The three Portgordon spies were taken to London for questioning. Their mission was a disaster from start to finish. The spies, two men and a woman, were landed from a German seaplane into a little boat and had to row ashore on the north-east coast of Scotland. But the bicycles they were supposed to use fell into the sea.

They decided to take the train to London but a sharp station-master spotted them and two were arrested. One man got as far as Edinburgh before he was caught. In prison he asked for the apples from his case. The police refused because they knew they'd be poisoned. The spy lived to give up all his secrets.